# Fire Trucks

Julie Murray

Abdo

MY COMMUNITY: VEHICLES

Kids

**abdopublishing.com**

Published by Abdo Kids, a division of ABDO, PO Box 398166, Minneapolis, Minnesota 55439.
Copyright © 2016 by Abdo Consulting Group, Inc. International copyrights reserved in all countries.
No part of this book may be reproduced in any form without written permission from the publisher.

Printed in the United States of America, North Mankato, Minnesota.

102015
012016

THIS BOOK CONTAINS
RECYCLED MATERIALS

Photo Credits: iStock, Shutterstock

Production Contributors: Teddy Borth, Jennie Forsberg, Grace Hansen

Design Contributors: Candice Keimig, Dorothy Toth


Library of Congress Control Number: 2015941782

Cataloging-in-Publication Data

Murray, Julie.
 Fire trucks / Julie Murray.
   p. cm. -- (My community: vehicles)
ISBN 978-1-68080-129-3
Includes index.
1. Fire engines--Juvenile literature.    I. Title.
629.225--dc23
                        2015941782

# Table of Contents

# Fire Truck

Dan sees a big truck.

It is red. It is a fire truck!

It has loud sirens.

Its lights flash.

It is going to a fire.

9

The firemen ride in the **cab**.

The truck has ladders.

The fireman climbs up high.

13

The truck has hoses.

The fireman sprays the water.

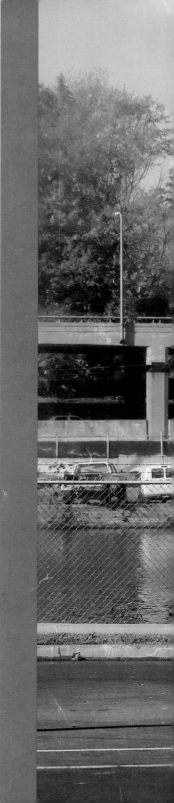

The firemen are in the **bucket**.

They put out the fire.

17

The fire truck is at the station.

It is ready for the next fire!

Have you seen a fire truck?

# Parts of a Fire Truck

cab

ladder

hose

lights

# Glossary

**bucket**
sometimes connected to the top of the ladder. It holds the firefighters and keeps them safe.

**cab**
where the driver sits in the fire truck.

# Index

# abdokids.com

Use this code to log on to abdokids.com and access crafts, games, videos, and more!

Abdo Kids Code:
## MFK1293